Every new generation of children is enthralled by the famous stories in our Well Loved Tales series. Younger ones love to have the story read to them. Older children will enjoy the exciting stories in an easy-to-read text.

British Library Cataloguing in Publication Data

Southgate, Vera
  Goldilocks and the three bears.—Rev ed.
  I. Title   II. Russell, Chris
  III. Series
  823'.914[J]
  ISBN 0-7214-1173-8

Revised edition

Published by Ladybird Books Ltd Loughborough Leicestershire UK
Ladybird Books Inc Auburn Maine 04210 USA

Printed in England

Goldilocks
and the
Three Bears

retold by VERA SOUTHGATE MA BCom

illustrated by CHRIS RUSSELL

Ladybird Books

Once upon a time there were three
bears who lived in a little house
in a wood. Father Bear was a very
big bear. Mother Bear was a
medium sized bear, and Baby Bear
was just a tiny little bear.

One morning, Mother Bear cooked some porridge for breakfast. She put it into three bowls. There was

a very big bowl for Father Bear,
a medium sized bowl for Mother
Bear and a tiny little bowl for
Baby Bear.

The porridge was very hot,

so the three bears went for a walk

in the wood while it was cooling.

At the edge of the wood, in another little house, there lived a little girl. Her golden hair was so long that she could sit on it and everyone called her Goldilocks.

That morning, Goldilocks was
walking in the wood.

Soon she came to the little house where the three bears lived. The door was open and she peeped inside. No one was there so Goldilocks walked in, which was a very naughty thing to do.

She saw the three bowls of porridge on the table. Goldilocks felt hungry so she tasted the porridge in the very big bowl. But it was too hot!

Next she tasted the porridge in the medium sized bowl. That was too lumpy!

But when she tasted the porridge in
the tiny little bowl, it was just right
and Goldilocks ate it all up.

Then Goldilocks saw three chairs.
There was a very big chair, a
medium sized chair and a tiny little
chair.

She sat in the very big chair. But it was too high!

She sat in the medium sized chair. It was too hard!

Then she sat in the tiny little chair. That was just right!

But the tiny little chair wasn't
strong enough to hold Goldilocks.
It began to crack, then it broke!

And Goldilocks landed with a
bump on the floor.

Goldilocks picked herself up and went to see what else she could find.

She went upstairs and looked into the bedroom. There she saw three beds. There was a very big bed, a medium sized bed and a tiny little bed.

Goldilocks climbed up onto the

very big bed. But it was too hard!

She tried the medium sized bed. It was too soft.

Then she lay down on the tiny little
bed. That was just right and soon
Goldilocks was fast asleep.

After a while the three bears came
home for breakfast. Father Bear
looked at his very big bowl and
said in a very loud voice,
"Someone's been eating my
porridge."

Then Mother Bear looked at her
medium sized bowl. "Someone's
been eating my porridge," she said
in a medium sized voice.

Baby Bear looked at his tiny little bowl. "Someone's been eating my porridge and they've eaten it all up!" he cried in a tiny little voice.

The three bears looked round the
room. Father Bear looked at his
very big chair. "Someone's been
sitting in my chair," he said in
a very loud voice.

Mother Bear looked at her medium sized chair. "Someone's been sitting in my chair," she said in a medium sized voice.

Baby Bear looked at his tiny little chair. "Someone's been sitting in my chair... and they've broken it!" he cried in a tiny little voice.

Then the three bears went upstairs
into the bedroom. Father Bear
looked at his very big bed.

"Someone's been lying on my bed," he roared.

Mother Bear looked at her medium sized bed. "Someone's been lying on my bed," she said in a medium sized voice.

Baby Bear looked at his tiny little
bed.

"Here she is!" he cried, making
his tiny little voice as loud as he
could. "Here is the naughty little
girl who's eaten my porridge and
broken my chair! Here she is!"

At the sound of their voices,

Goldilocks woke up.

When she saw the three bears she
was so frightened that she jumped
out of bed, ran down the stairs,
out of the house and into the
wood as fast as she could.

By the time the three bears reached the door, Goldilocks was gone.

From that day on the three bears
never saw Goldilocks again, and
they lived happily ever after.